FINDERS
KEEPERS

D0048199

FINDERS KEEPERS

Melanie McFarlane

ORCA BOOK PUBLISHERS

Published in Canada and the United States in 2021 by Orca Book Publishers.
orcabook.com

Library and Archives Canada Cataloguing in Publication
Title: Finders keepers / Melanie McFarlane.
Names: McFarlane, Melanie, author.
Series: Orca currents.
Description: Series statement: Orca currents
Identifiers: Canadiana (print) 2020027046x | Canadiana (ebook) 20200270575 |
ISBN 9781459827691 (softcover) | ISBN 9781459827707 (PDF) |
ISBN 9781459827714 (EPUB)
Classification: LCC PS8625.F375 F56 2021 | DDC jc813/.6—dc23

Library of Congress Control Number: 2020939208

Summary: In this high-interest accessible novel for middle readers,
Macy discovers a mermaid in the prairie lake near her home.

Orca Book Publishers is committed to reducing the consumption of
nonrenewable resources in the making of our books. We make
every effort to use materials that support a sustainable future.

Orca Book Publishers gratefully acknowledges the support for its publishing
programs provided by the following agencies: the Government of Canada,
the Canada Council for the Arts and the Province of British Columbia
through the BC Arts Council and the Book Publishing Tax Credit.

Design by Ella Collier
Cover design by Ella Collier
Cover artwork by Getty Images/Yuri_Arcurs
Edited by Tanya Trafford
Author photo by Michelle Heisler

Printed and bound in Canada.

24 23 22 21 • 1 2 3 4

For Emily, my adventurer, and all the

readers in search of buried treasure.

Chapter One

I dug deep into the muddy sand. I was looking for treasure at the bottom of the lake. But the more I dug, the darker the water got. Then something soft touched my foot. I froze. What was it? A weed? Or, worse, a hungry fish? I was a treasure hunter, not a diver. I needed to get out of here!

As soon as my head popped out of the water, I gasped for air. I was at the very far end of the marked swimming area. I thought again about what could be moving around below me. Why had I swum out so far? I knew if Mom were here, she'd tell me to just take a breath, that my active imagination was always working overtime. But she was at work right now. She is a park ranger for Buffalo Pound Provincial Park. That's why we live here.

I love living at the lake. I can ride my bike anywhere I want to go. I have hills to explore. And my best friend, Sam, lives close by, so we can hang out most days. But the lake water hides a ton of scaly creatures that make me nervous. Have you ever seen a fish up close? Their big eyes, spiky fins and sharp teeth make them look like monsters.

"Hurry up, Macy!" Sam called from the shore. He was standing next to my little brother. Real nice. They left me alone out here to be fish food.

I looked around, trying to figure out the fastest way out of the lake. Old Lady Wilson's dock was to the right. In front of me was the beach. To my left were tall reeds—they were a bit closer, but I hate the feel of moving through them.

Something soft touched my foot again. The creature had found me! This time it grabbed on to my toes!

"Ahh!" I screamed, kicking my feet furiously. It wasn't letting go!

I swam as fast as I could toward the beach. When I reached the shallow water, I tried to stand but slipped on the thing attached to my foot. I fell back into the water and grabbed at my toes. It was just a chunk of lake weed. I laughed, but then remembered that leeches and other creepy crawlers love to hide in lake weed.

I stood up quickly. I looked down at my feet to make sure there was nothing near them. That's when I spotted something sparkly under the water. I had to investigate. Finding things is kind of my thing.

I started digging carefully like I'd learned from my handbook, *Treasure Hunting 101*. Rule number one: Always protect the scene.

My fingers found something solid. It felt like a bottle. I pulled it out of the sand and held it over my head like a trophy. I had found the first treasure of the day!

"Hey!" Sam called out. "What's that?" He ran into the water and stood next to me.

"Aw," said my little brother, joining us. "It's just a bottle."

"Hang on," I said. Something clinked inside the bottle.

I flipped the bottle over. With a *THUNK*, a blob of wet sand fell out. Stuck inside the bottle was a beautiful pink shell that glimmered. I tried to shake it out.

"Whoa, that's cool," Sam said. "I've never seen a shell like that before."

"Maybe it's from the ocean!" my brother said.

"That's impossible, Bug," I said. My brother is eight years old. His real name is Ben. Mom thinks I call him Bug because he likes creepy crawlers. But really it's because he's so annoying, a real pain in my butt. I always have to babysit him.

"Is not," Bug said. He crossed his arms.

I grunted. The closest ocean is more than a thousand miles away. But Bug had a point. This shell did not look like any of the brown clamshells I'd found at the bottom of the lake.

I shrugged. "Lost treasure?"

We made our way back to the beach. Sam and Bug followed me up to the rocky ledge where we'd left our bags and bikes. Close to Mrs. Wilson's cabin, it was the perfect place to stash our stuff, away from the crowds of people on the beach.

Bug pushed between us. "How did that big shell get in that tiny opening anyway?" he asked.

"Beat it, Bug." I peered into the bottle. I'd seen a ship in a bottle before, down at the Treasure Trove, the local general store. But someone had built that boat inside the bottle, piece by piece. Bug was right. How did a shell get inside this one?

"But I want to see," said Bug.

He grabbed at the bottle. I lost my grip, and the bottle fell out of my hands. It smashed against the rocky shore. Glass shot everywhere, like sparks at a campfire. The shell slid between two rocks, just out of reach.

"Bug!" I yelled. "Look what you did."

Bug stepped back, crossing his arms again and pinching his lips together. "I'm going to tell Mom you're not being nice."

"I'll tell her you smashed a bottle," I said, trying to dig out the shell. "And here, of all places."

Right on cue, a screech came from the front porch of the cabin. "What are you kids doing down there?" Old Lady Wilson stood there, shaking her cane at us.

"Run!" I pulled the shell free, threw it in my bag and jumped on my bike.

I didn't wait for Bug or Sam. I kicked down the pedal and took off. I didn't stop until I got to the top of Crow's Hill. Soon Sam caught up to me, both of us huffing and puffing.

We had escaped. We had the shell. Everything was perfect.

"Wait," I said. "Where's Bug?"

Chapter Two

"I can't see him," I said, scanning Old Lady Wilson's yard from the top of the hill.

"You should be happy. Now we're Bug-free," Sam said. He had taken out his soccer ball and was bouncing it on his knees.

Sam doesn't have a little brother. All he babysits is his soccer ball. He carries it in his backpack all the time.

"We have to go find him," I said.

We walked our bikes back down the hill and hid them in the ditch by Old Lady Wilson's place. Then Sam and I crept up to the long line of bushes that separated the beach from her yard, making our way to the shore.

We could see Old Lady Wilson on the other side of the bushes, poking around the rocks with a stick. Her back was to us, and her long silver braid peeked out under her hat. She was muttering to herself.

"What's she doing?" Sam whispered louder than he should have.

I brought a finger to my lips. "Shh."

The old woman's voice drifted between the leaves. "The beast," she mumbled. "I can't let the beast find it."

What was she looking for? I leaned forward to try to hear better, but something startled me in the bushes beside us. I froze. Was it the *beast*? The leaves stirred again, and then Bug stumbled out.

"What were you doing in there?" I asked, relieved.

Bug shrugged, pulling leaves from his hair. "You took off too fast, and I hid so the lady wouldn't keep yelling at me."

"Sheesh, Bug." I shook my head. "You need to stay close. Mom would have killed me if I'd lost you." Bug just stared at me. "Go get your bike," I said. "It's time to go hunting."

We biked back to the picnic area. It's a treasure hunter's dream. My plan was to find a big treasure before Mom made us move to the city for work. A big treasure meant money, which might convince Mom to stay.

"Look over there!" Bug said. Before I could see what he was talking about, he ran off toward the tall grass that separated the picnic area from the lake.

"Should we follow him?" Sam asked.

I shook my head. "If Bug is going to leave the hunt, then he gives up his share of the treasure."

I searched the picnic tables—on top and underneath—but they were empty. In fact, the last people who had eaten here were so clean they had even wiped down the tables before they left. Mom would be happy we were doing our part to keep the park clean.

"Bummer," Sam said, reaching for his soccer ball.

"I better see where Bug went," I said as I headed toward the tall grass.

I pushed through the grass. It was so high it reached my chin, and it was full of cattails and weeds. The grass ended at a tiny hill that led down to the sandy beach. But this wasn't a tourist-friendly beach. Rocks and broken clamshells were scattered everywhere. Hungry seagulls often stopped here for afternoon snacks.

Bug was behind a log, peeking at something down the shore. Maybe he'd found a treasure.

"What's up, Bug?" I asked.

"Shh," he said, handing me the binoculars. "It's a sora rail. It's a waterbird. It's shy. Don't scare it away."

I knelt and looked through the binoculars. I could see a small bird with a yellow beak hopping along the beach. "Boring. Birds do nothing but eat, fly and poop."

If Sam was here, he would have giggled. I can always get him going with poop talk. Bug didn't even crack a smile.

"You don't get it." He tried to grab the binoculars back from me.

Bug is right. I'm not obsessed with wildlife like he is. It *is* pretty cool how much he knows about the different kinds of animals around here. But I would never tell him that.

Leaning back against the log, I used the binoculars to scan the beach for anything that looked promising. Parts of the hill had broken away. At its base were piles of dried-up lake weed. Something in one of the piles caught my eye. A wallet!

"Treasure!" I jumped up and ran. I grabbed the wallet and waved it in the air. A shiny silver pen fell out and landed on my shoe.

Sam leaped out of the grass above me. "Cool pen!" he said.

I kicked it over to him. Treasure-hunting rule number two: Always share with your team.

Bug joined us. He shot me one of his disapproving looks. "You can't keep that!" he said.

"Finders keepers," I said, putting the wallet in my backpack. "It's the law of the land."

"But it's *wrong*," Bug said.

I rolled my eyes. Bug is four years younger than me. But he acts like he knows everything. "We'll turn it in at the store like we always do," I said. "Let's go."

Chapter Three

The Treasure Trove is part ice-cream shop, part general store. Locals just called it the Trove. And it has the best lost-and-found rule! If lost items aren't claimed in a week, the person who turned them in gets to keep them.

Drake McDaniel was behind the front counter. His hair was a mess. He looked like he had just gotten out of bed. He thinks he is so great and always makes fun of us. He claims he is a *master* treasure hunter. But I've never seen him find a single thing.

"Oh, look," Drake said. "The famous hunters are here. What junk did you bring in this time?"

"Is the Captain in?" I asked. The Captain is the owner and is the best part of visiting the store. He always has interesting stories to share about his days at sea.

"Ahoy, mateys!" The Captain's deep voice filled the room as he entered. "How goes the hunting?"

The Captain's broad shoulders and round belly shook as he laughed heartily. He always dresses the part, wearing a black-and-white captain's hat with gold trim, his long white hair tied back. A scruffy white beard covers his chin.

"We bring treasure," I said, placing the wallet on the counter. Sam lay the silver pen down too.

"Great work, mateys!" The Captain scooped up the wallet. "You'll be pleased to know that the owner of this here wallet has already filed a Missing report. You did good, kids. Right honorable!"

Well, I guess I would be happy if someone had found my wallet. Still, it was a bit disappointing to know I wasn't any closer to my goal. But then I remembered I had found something else today. "Hey," I asked, pointing to the bottle up on the shelf behind the counter. "How would someone get a shell *inside* a bottle?"

"A shell?" The Captain scratched his head. "I guess it would depend on what kind of shell you're talkin' about."

"It doesn't look like any shell we've ever seen," Bug said. "It's got pink and white stripes and is kind of sparkly. It looks like something that came from the ocean."

The Captain's eyebrows shot up. "A shell from the ocean? Now that's interesting. Show me." He leaned against the counter. "I did sail the Pacific for thirty-odd years, as you know. I could tell ye for sure if it's a saltwater shell or a freshwater one."

"Sure," I said, frowning at Bug as I pulled my bag off my shoulder and searched through it. When I found the shell, both Drake and the Captain leaned far over the countertop to see.

"Wow," Drake said. His eyes grew wide as he reached for the shell. "That is very cool. Where did you find this again?"

I yanked the shell out of Drake's reach and passed it to the Captain. "I didn't say," I replied.

The Captain whistled as he gently took the shell in his large, rough hands. "Well, I'll be. That there's a shell from the ocean, indeed!"

"Really?" I'd never seen the ocean, let alone held a shell from it. "How do you think it got into a bottle?"

"I think," the Captain said, turning the shell, over in his hands, "that someone must have wanted to protect it very much."

"Cool!" Sam said. "Is it worth anything?"

Drake leaned in close to the shell. "Look, Captain," he said. "It's broken." He seemed pleased.

"Oh dear," the Captain said, flipping the shell over. "You're right. There's a big piece missing. That will definitely affect its value."

"But that's all we've got," I said. "What if we found the other piece?"

Drake snorted. "You'll never find it."

"I don't think a broken shell is worth much, even if you glue it back together," the Captain said. "But you never know."

"I bet I can find it, Captain," Drake said.

The Captain just looked at him.

"No," I said. "*We'll* find it." There was no way I was letting Drake get his grubby hands on our treasure.

"In the meantime, if it's all right with you, I'll put the shell back here in the lost-and-found bin."

The Captain leaned forward and winked. "Just in case its owner comes looking for it."

I looked at the shell. Even though it was broken and probably wasn't worth much, for some reason it felt to me like my biggest find yet.

"Okay," I said. "But let me know if anyone asks about it."

"Will do, little lady. Drake, get these kids some ice cream to fuel their travels," the Captain said.

We left the store with our ice-cream cones. "Eat those somewhere else," Drake had snapped. "I'm not cleaning up after you." He is so nasty.

The sun was directly above our heads. Mom would be expecting us for lunch soon. We walked with our bikes until we had finished our cones, then raced home.

"We need to get back to Old Lady Wilson's after lunch," I said to Sam as we pulled up to my cabin.

Sam stopped his bike and put his foot on the ground to balance. "Why?"

"To find the missing part of the shell," I said. "It must have broken off when it fell on the rocks. I don't know why, but it feels important."

"Okay, but any way we can ditch some of our cargo?" He pointed his thumb behind me at Bug, pedaling furiously to catch up. I nodded, then turned and punched the SOLD sign posted in our front yard.

When I got inside, I saw that Mom had lunch all ready. She was sitting at the table. I like seeing her in her park ranger uniform. She looks important. Her light green button-up shirt has short sleeves with a badge on each side. A utility belt holds up her brown pants. That's where she carries her gun. Sometimes I forget Mom's job can be risky.

Bug and I sat down. I was a bit full from the ice cream, but we ate our sandwiches anyway. Bug told her about the weird bird he had seen on the beach. I didn't mention our little shell adventure. I wanted to keep it to myself a bit longer.

Mom got ready to go back to work. Before she left, she turned and said, "Macy, this afternoon I would like you and Bug to start packing up your bedrooms."

"What?" I nearly spit out my milk. "I don't want to start packing yet! We don't even have boxes."

"Macy," Mom said. "I don't have time to argue with you about this. It has to be done. I picked up some boxes this morning." She motioned to a pile of cardboard in the living room. "You can start by putting them together. Get Bug to help."

My thoughts went back to the shell in the bin at the Trove. Would I ever find a treasure big enough to make Mom want to stay at the lake?

"Fine," I said. "I can put the boxes together. But that's it."

After Mom left, I called Sam and told him our next hunt would have to wait until Mom got home from work. But at least we'd solved one problem—Bug could stay home.

Chapter Four

There were two things everyone knew about Old Lady Wilson. She had the best dock in town. And she didn't want anyone near her boathouse.

"Be back before dark," Mom said.

Sam and I hid our bikes on the other side of the road in front of the cabin. We were both dressed in dark colors. The lights from Mrs. Wilson's TV flashed through the cabin's main window. Perfect. She'd likely never even notice us.

As we got down to the rocks, I searched for the spot where we had dropped the bottle. But every rock had the same gray pattern as the next.

"I think we were over there," Sam said, pointing toward the boathouse. Like always, he had his soccer ball tucked under one arm.

"We weren't that close," I said. "Keep looking." I motioned to Sam. "It has to be here somewhere."

Sam moved toward the dock. "Look what I found!" he said. He held up a long stick and walked toward me. As he got closer I could see it was a walking stick that looked like it had been carved from a tree branch. Oh no.

"Where did you find this?" I asked.

Sam pointed toward the dock.

"It's the old lady's cane! She must be out here." I ducked low and looked out at the lake. Sure enough, a couple of voices floated our way.

We tiptoed toward the boathouse, listening carefully. The closer we got to the back corner, the louder the voices were.

The first voice was Mrs. Wilson's. "I'm worried. How will we find it now?"

"Everything will be fine," said another woman. I didn't recognize her voice. She sounded much younger. "Don't worry, Joy."

Joy? That was the old lady's name? Sam and I looked at each other, our eyes wide. I tried not to giggle. That name was far too fluffy and sweet for someone so grumpy.

"I've been trying to read up on the Beast—"

"You won't find it in your books," the other woman said. "It's a monster."

Joy grunted. "Monsters come from somewhere."

"Some would call *me* a monster." The other woman laughed.

"That's not funny, MerKay. Someone needs to watch out for you—you don't belong here."

What did she mean by that? Their voices dropped too low for us to hear anything more. I leaned around the corner but slipped on the edge of the deck and hit the railing. With a *craaack*, it broke apart. I reached for Sam's hand, but it was too late. I fell face first into the lake and started to sink.

The chilly water was dark. I couldn't figure out which way was up. My lungs hurt. I needed air!

Suddenly two hands grabbed me under my arms and pulled me out of the water. I sputtered and coughed up lake water as my rescuer pushed me onto the dock. I turned back to say thank you, but no one was there.

"Who's down there?" Joy called out.

I looked up and saw the old lady standing at the spot where I had broken the railing.

Sam appeared in the water next to me. "Come on!" he said. "We need to get out of here."

"Don't move, you hooligans!" Joy yelled. "I'm coming down there!"

I slid back into the water and followed Sam toward the beach. I stayed underwater as long as I could and then pushed myself to the surface. I had reached the beach. That had to be a lake record for breath holding!

"My soccer ball," Sam said, throwing himself onto the sand. "I dropped it near Old Lady Wilson's boathouse when you fell in. How will I get it back?"

I sat on the sand next to Sam. The sky was darker now, but we were safe. "Come over first thing in the morning. I still want to find that missing piece of shell. But I'll help you find your soccer ball too. I promise. I owe you one for saving me back there."

"What, from Old Lady Wilson?" Sam asked. "I mean, from *Joy*?" We both chuckled.

"No," I said, shaking the water from my hair. "When you helped me up onto the dock after I fell in."

"Uh, Macy," Sam said. "You must have hit your head. I didn't help you. I was so freaked out, I hid.

When Old Lady Wilson got too close to me, I jumped into the water."

"If it wasn't you, then who?" I asked.

But before Sam could answer, we both heard someone crashing through the bushes. Joy!

"You're not getting away this time!" she called out.

Sam and I ran to the picnic area. There was a row of evergreens at the far end. They gave us cover to run to the road without being spotted. Once there we ducked into the ditch and kept our heads low.

When we reached our bikes, Sam whispered, "Whew! That was a close one!"

"Yeah. See you in the morning? We have to complete our mission."

Sam nodded and headed for home.

When I got into the house, Mom was in the kitchen. She was wearing her uniform.

"Perfect timing, Macy," she said. "I've got to run to the bison pen. There's been some vandalism. I'll be about an hour, and I need you to watch Ben."

The bison pen was a huge fenced area about a ten-minute drive from our cabin. Real bison lived there, and it was set up so visitors could learn about the history of the area.

I watched Mom drive away from the cabin. My heart was still pounding from our narrow escape. The sun was hidden behind the hills now. Shadows stretched across our yard. I shuddered. They looked like long scraggly fingers reaching toward our cabin.

Chapter Five

The next day I waited for Sam on the front step. When he showed up, he had his shirt on inside out. He was super fidgety, and he couldn't stop yawning.

"It's no use," Sam said. "I'm never getting my soccer ball back."

I shook my head. Treasure-hunting rule number three: Never say never. "I've got an idea," I said. "But it requires one more treasure hunter."

In the backyard, Bug was snuggled up in our hammock, reading a book. Sam and I each took a side so he couldn't escape.

"We need your help," I said, almost choking on the last word. I couldn't remember ever asking Bug for help.

Bug peeked over the top of his book, his brows squished together. "What for?"

"It's top secret," I said. "Treasure-hunting business."

"No thanks," Bug said. "The last time I went hunting with you two, it wasn't any fun."

"Please," Sam begged. "I lost my soccer ball. And it is going to be very tricky to get it back."

"Tricky how?" Bug asked.

"It's a three-person job," I said. "We'll even give you all the treasures we find. Deal?"

Bug sat up. "All the treasures?"

I nodded, holding out my hand. I knew we wouldn't find much. We were going straight to the boathouse, then back again. It was a quick job.

"Deal," Bug said, abandoning his book and shaking my hand.

We started hiking back to Crow's Hill. But then Bug clued in. "Wait, are we going back to Mrs. Wilson's cabin?"

I shook my head. "Not the cabin, Bug. The boathouse."

"Are you serious?" he asked. "After what happened?"

I took my little brother by the shoulders. "Bug, you shook on it. We have a deal. There's no going back now."

His mouth dropped open, but no words came out. Then he pushed my hands away and crossed his arms.

"Fine," he said. "But if anything goes wrong, I'm telling Mom."

Telling Mom. The biggest threat of all. But there was no time to argue. Sam wouldn't survive another day without his beloved soccer ball, and I needed to find that missing shell piece. I led my team down the hill, across the road and to the edge of the bushes.

"Let's do this," I said.

I put Bug on lookout while Sam and I sneaked to the boathouse. My directions were simple. If Bug saw Mrs. Wilson, he'd hold up his binoculars and pretend he had spotted a rare bird near her property. That way he'd keep her attention on him instead of us.

As we neared the boathouse, I picked up my pace. We were only ten feet away—nine—eight—

"What are you up to?" Mrs. Wilson's voice yelled from behind us.

I ran the last stretch and hid around the corner of the boathouse. Sam practically fell on top of me.

"I'm following a wood thrush," I heard Bug say. I had to give the kid credit. He put on a good show.

"Interesting," she replied. "I've never seen one up close." I could see her standing beside Bug now, both of them looking up into the sky. I let out a long breath. We were in the clear!

We quickly searched the bushes where Sam had been standing the night before. There was no sign of the soccer ball.

"Oh no!" said Sam.

"What?"

He had his hands on a dusty window, peering inside. "My soccer ball! It's *inside* the boathouse!"

"Well, let's get it then," I replied. The door was locked. I pulled at the old padlock, but it didn't budge.

"What now?" Sam asked.

I crawled to the broken railing and looked down at the water. It was the last place I wanted to go, but we had no choice. The only way we could get into the boathouse was to swim in underneath.

"Follow me," I said.

Very carefully I stepped into the water. It was just as cold as it had been the night before.

Just as we got under the boathouse, I felt something brush past my face. *Not again!* This time it didn't feel like weeds. It felt more like a fish tail.

I scrambled up onto the boathouse floor. Sam was already making his way to the shelves on the far wall.

I looked down at the water. I swore there was something following me. That feathery thing brushing across my face. I was sure it was attached to—

"Aha!" Sam said, making me jump. He reached up to a shelf and pulled down his soccer ball.

"Hey, check this place out," I said, moving away from the water. A desk sat against one wall. Above it were photos of Mrs. Wilson, taken from all around the world. A bookshelf sat against another wall, with titles like *Treasures of the Ancient World* and *Kessler's Guide to Mythical Creatures*. There was even a book called *A History of Buffalo Pound Lake*. But the coolest of all was on her desk—several large shiny scales, as big as my hand.

The boards creaked outside the boathouse door. I held a finger to my lips. If the old lady caught us, we were dead. I tiptoed back to the water. But before I could jump in, something moved below the surface.

The boathouse door swung open. Mrs. Wilson stood there, holding on tightly to Bug's arm. She pulled him inside the boathouse, closing the door behind them.

"I've caught you red-handed, Macy Kramer!" she said. "Now give me back my shell!"

Her shell? Did she mean the one we'd found the day before? "We don't have your shell," I said.

"I know it was you," she said, pointing her finger at me. "I found the broken glass yesterday, and now my shell is missing. I also know you returned to the scene of the crime last night."

She pointed to the ball in Sam's hands, proof of our failed adventure.

"But she's telling the truth!" Bug cried. "We don't have the shell."

A splash of water, followed by a deep growl, made me jump again. I spun around and found a strange creature staring up at me from the water. Green scales covered its body, spiky fins stuck out from its head, and its wide smile revealed a row of sharp teeth.

All my fears about monsters in the lake were true!

Chapter Six

"They aren't lying, Joy," the creature said, pulling itself from the water onto the edge of the dock. I noticed that it had a large fish tail instead of legs. "I checked their pockets."

"Are you a—" I couldn't finish. I was in shock. A lake creature covered in scales sat in front of me.

"A mermaid?" it asked. Its green scales reflected tiny lights all over the boathouse.

"It was you," I said, "wasn't it? You're the one who helped me onto the dock last night."

"You're welcome," the mermaid said, winking at me.

"Whoa!" Sam said. "Wait a minute. You're saying you're a *real* mermaid?"

"That's—impossible," I said. "This is a freshwater lake. It isn't even that deep. How can you survive?"

"With the help of friends." The mermaid nodded at Joy.

I turned toward Mrs. Wilson. "You? But you don't even like other people in your yard, let alone near your boathouse."

Joy huffed. "What I don't like is people smashing glass on my beach or breaking into my boathouse. And don't think I haven't heard what you kids call me. I have a name, you know."

"Yes, Mrs. Wilson," I said, looking down at my sneakers.

She leaned in so close I could have counted the wrinkles on her face. And there were a *lot*. She surprised me with what she said next. "Perhaps there's hope for you after all. You can call me Joy."

I shook my head. This was just too much to take in. Old Lady Wilson—Joy—was secretly hiding a mermaid in her boathouse! And she was being nice to me!

"I have a name too," said the mermaid. "It's MerKay."

"Why doesn't anyone else know you exist?" I asked.

"Watch this," MerKay said. Her scales shimmered and changed color until finally she was the same shade of brown as the inside of the boathouse.

"It's easy to hide when no one is looking for you," she said.

"I've been trying to get MerKay home," Joy said. "But it's been tricky."

"The Beast kidnapped me," MerKay said. "Snatched me right out of the ocean and brought me here. I was kept captive in a large moving tank, surrounded by creatures unlike anything I'd ever seen before."

"So what's keeping you here now?" I asked. "Why not just get Old—I mean, Joy to take you home?"

"It's not that easy," MerKay said. "The Beast took my shell when he caught me. I need that shell to find my family again." She looked down for a moment. I realized she wasn't a monster at all.

"When I escaped the Beast," MerKay continued, "I tried to take my shell back, but it fell and broke into two pieces. I only had time to grab one before I escaped into the lake."

"I kept that piece in a bottle tied up under my dock," Joy said. "But the rope must have snapped. I didn't even realize it was missing until I found the broken glass on the shore."

"Macy found a shell in a bottle yesterday," Bug said. "But it was missing a piece."

"That's my shell!" Joy said. "Where is it now?"

I hesitated. "Um—it's at the Trove."

"We'll get it back for you," Sam added.

"I can't let you leave until you swear you won't reveal our secret," Joy said. "MerKay's survival depends on it."

"I swear," Sam said, holding his hand in the air.

"Mom says we shouldn't swear," Bug said. "But I promise not to tell anyone. I *promise!*"

But I hesitated. This was the kind of treasure I'd been looking for all summer. A real live mermaid. Not a single place on Earth could say they had one. A mermaid would put our little lake on the map as a top tourist spot. Tourist money meant more jobs. Would Mom want to move away if we could be famous? We could stay at the lake forever!

"Come on, Macy," Bug said, looking up at me. "We need to help the shiny lady."

Sam raised an eyebrow. It wasn't about Bug's comment.

I bit my lip. I knew what the right thing to do was. Why was it so hard? I dug into my backpack and pulled out my most prized possession, my treasure-hunting handbook. Putting my hand on the cover, I said, "I swear on all that a treasure hunter holds dear to do everything I can to protect MerKay."

Joy opened the door to the boathouse and allowed us to pass. The three of us ran all the way to the Trove. We had found a real mermaid!

When we got to the store, the *Closed* sign was hanging in the window. I knocked on the door. No one answered. I could see the Captain's old pickup truck parked along the side. Maybe he was still here.

"Let's look around back," Sam said.

The store backed onto a small beach with a boat dock known for its diving board, which looked like a pirate's gangplank. When the Captain had taken over the store, he'd closed the dock to the public, roping it off so no one could swim there.

I peered through the screen door. It was too dark to see anything inside. But maybe he was in there. I knew there was a bedroom in the back that he referred to as "the Captain's quarters."

"Captain?" I called out. "Are you there?"

A muffled cry came from the other side of the door. I yanked open the screen door and stepped inside.

"What are you doing?" Bug hissed behind me.

"Someone needs help," I whispered.

The Captain's room was empty. There was nothing but a bed, a trunk and another door.

Someone cried out from behind that door. Then I heard a large crash. I pushed the door open and almost knocked over the Captain.

"What the—" the Captain began. "Macy? Sam? Bug? What are you doing in my bedroom?"

"We heard a noise!" I said. "I thought you were in trouble."

"Oh," the Captain said, squinting past us. "I'm just moving this large fish tank out of storage."

"What for?" Bug asked.

"You know that shell you brought me?" the Captain said. "I think the lake has a lot of hidden treasures in it. Maybe you can help me find more. And where better to show off interesting finds than at the Trove? It would be a great tourist attraction."

My face dropped. The Captain would be disappointed to hear that we needed the shell back.

"What? I thought treasure hunters like you three would be excited to put your findings on exhibit," the Captain said. "You'll get to keep your claim on each, of course."

"It is a great idea," I said, thinking about all the cool rocks, shells and other treasures we'd found in the past. "But we need that shell back."

The Captain looked surprised. "Oh, really? Did you find its owner?"

"Sort of," Bug said.

"No," Sam said at the same time.

The Captain frowned.

"We'll replace it with something really cool," I added. "We promise."

"Okay then," the Captain said. "Follow me."

He led the three of us to the front of the store. He ducked behind the counter and started rooting around in some bins. "I know I put it here somewhere. Hmmm. Or maybe it was over here. No. What the—?" The Captain stood up, his face red and strands of his long hair escaping its ponytail. "It's gone. I don't understand."

"What?" I said. "Are you sure you didn't move it?"

"I know it was here last night when I closed the store," the Captain said. "That's what gave me the idea to pull out the old fish tank."

"But it's really imp—" Bug began.

Sam elbowed him in the ribs, cutting him off.

The Captain narrowed his gaze at Bug, then turned to Sam and finally to me. "Is there something you kids aren't telling me?"

"No, uh, we just really wanted it back," I said. "You know, it's not every day you find such a cool shell. And, like you said, it's probably not worth much."

The Captain nodded in agreement. "I'll check with Drake when he's back. He's out on a hunt right now. That shell has to be around here somewhere."

"Call us as soon as you find it," Bug said.

"Deal," the Captain said. "Whoa! Look at the time. I better get a move on. Oh, and I'm sorry to tell you kids, but I'm out of ice cream until further notice."

"No ice cream?" I said. Could this day get any worse?

"There was a problem with the supplier," the Captain said. "But I hope we'll get it sorted out soon."

He unlocked the front door, and the three of us shuffled outside. How would we break the news to MerKay? Her shell, the only thing that could help her get back home, was missing.

Chapter Seven

MerKay was not there when we got back to Joy's cabin to tell them the news. "The Beast must have stolen it," said Joy. "I bet it knows MerKay is close."

Bug, Sam and I marched back to my cabin for lunch. Mom's Jeep was parked in our driveway. She must have finished work early.

"Do you think it was the Beast who took the shell?" Bug asked me before we went into the house. He looked frightened.

"Maybe," I said. "We'd have to find the Beast first to know for sure though."

"How are we ever going to find a monster around here?" Sam asked.

"Hey, kids," Mom said as we walked in. "Why so glum?"

"We lost something," Bug said, setting his binoculars on the table as he sat down.

"Something really important," Sam added, sitting next to him.

Mom brought over a plate of sandwiches and joined us at the table. "Was it valuable?" she asked.

"Priceless," I said.

Mom stopped eating. "Don't tell me you were digging in my jewelry box."

"Mom!" I rolled my eyes. "No. It was a special shell."

"One of a kind," Sam added.

"Magical," Bug said. I kicked him under the table. He scowled at me.

"I'm sorry to hear that," Mom said. "Maybe you can find another treasure this afternoon. I have to work later, but I thought we could do something fun for couple of hours. Maybe go out to the bison pen together and then swing by the flats."

Bug squealed. The flats were the best spot in the area for bird-watching, and he loved going there. I thought Mom's plan was boring until something occurred to me. Maybe some of the signs at the bison pen would have historical clues that could lead us to the Beast. Maybe there was a reason it had brought MerKay to Buffalo Pound Lake.

"Good idea, Mom," I said, "We've got some hunting to do."

She smiled. "Great. Sam, call your mom and make sure it's okay," she said.

When we arrived at the bison pen, I climbed the steps to the lookout two at a time. By the time I reached the third level, I was out of breath. The bison pen stretched out below, so big that I couldn't see the back fence. I had been here many times, although I had hardly ever seen bison.

A sign on the top level explained how the hills around the lake had been used by hunters to trap bison for food. I skimmed through the text, but I couldn't find anything that would lead us to the Beast.

"Any luck?" I asked Sam and Bug, joining them at the railing.

"Not one bison," Sam said, passing me Bug's binoculars.

I held up the binoculars and scanned the pen. There were hills, trees and grass as far as the eye could see. Sam was right. No bison.

"You know," Bug said, "there's no way a bison could be the Beast."

"I know." I sighed. "I just hoped that we'd find information here to help MerKay."

"Sorry, kids," Mom said. "I should have brought you out with me yesterday There were quite a few roaming around."

"Why were you called out here again?" I asked as I scanned the trail that ran alongside the pen.

"Vandals cut the fence," she said. "Luckily, someone spotted the gap before any bison got out."

"Did you get it fixed?" Sam asked.

"Just a patch job for now," Mom said. "A new fence will go up later today."

Hmm. A large hole in the fence. I wondered why it was needed. That sounded like a mystery for a treasure hunter. I passed the binoculars back to Bug.

"Mom, can we go to the flats now?" asked Bug.

"Ugh, Mom," I said. "Do we have to? Sam and I were hoping we could hike down to the bison trail. I want to see the big hole."

Bug's eyes grew large. "But I want to see the birds!"

"We don't have time to do both, I'm afraid," Mom said. "Anyway, not much to see. The hole's been patched. And it's not safe for hikers until it's properly secured."

"Then we'll take the trail on the other side," I said. "We won't go anywhere near the hole. I promise."

Mom gave me a stern look, then turned to Sam. "What about you, Sam? The flats or the bison trail?"

Sam looked sideways at me. I gave him my best stare down. "Um, the bison trail, I guess."

Mom looked at Bug, who had his arms crossed, and sighed. "Okay, why don't we split up? You two go check out the trail, and I'll take Ben to the flats. But you have to promise to meet me back at the Jeep in one hour. Deal?"

"Deal!" I said, already making for the stairs.

"And stay away from the north fence!" Mom called after us.

Sam and I walked along the path between the bison pen and the lake. From the lookout, it was just over a mile to get to the trail. Mom was smart. It would take us almost exactly one hour to hike there and back. She had left us no time for looking for clues. But I didn't plan to go all the way to the trail. I was determined to check the north fence. Sam and I would find the hole, hunt around and then head back to the Jeep in time to meet Mom.

"Why did you want to hike so bad?" Sam asked. "Shouldn't we be looking for the missing shell?"

"Think about it, Sam," I said. "Someone cut a large hole in the bison pen just after we found the shell. That sounds fishy."

"Maybe it was one of those animal-rights groups," Sam said. "You know, Free the Bison or something."

"Nah," I said. "The bison are protected here. I think someone was trying to hide something inside the pen. But maybe they got caught before they could cover their tracks."

"Hide what?" Sam asked.

"I don't know," I said, motioning to the fence. "But if they needed a hole this big, it must be something special."

Even though a new sheet of chain link covered up the damage, the outline of the hole stood out like a secret door.

"That's bigger than a bison," Sam said. "What do you think they were trying to do?"

I looked down the hill toward the marsh. Did the vandals have a boat? Why else would they need to cut the fence on this side of the lake? None of it made any sense.

Up ahead a line of trees blocked the view. If I was going to hide something, that would be the perfect spot.

"Sam," I called out. "Follow me."

"Oh man," he said. "Are we still hiking?"

"No," I said. "We're treasure hunting. What if the vandal was trying to get something out of the pen?

Remember how MerKay told us she'd been kept in a tank when she first arrived at the lake?"

"Right," Sam said. "And there were creatures all around unlike anything she'd ever seen before."

"Yes!" I said. "At first I thought she meant humans. But I bet it was the bison. What if the Beast was keeping her hidden somewhere inside the pen? And now he's getting ready to hunt down MerKay again," I said as we approached the row of trees. "Look!"

An old cube van with the faint logo of a seafood company on its side was hidden behind the trees. I tiptoed toward the van, careful to keep my head low.

"Maybe we should call someone for help," Sam said. He looked nervous.

"And tell them what?" I asked. "That we found an old abandoned van?"

I took a deep breath and reached for the driver's-door handle. Treasure-hunting rule number four: Courage is your best tool. The door creaked on its rusty hinges, and for a moment I almost slammed the door shut and ran away. But I held back my fear and opened the door all the way.

I pulled myself up to the driver's seat. *Eww!* It smelled like rotten fish inside. I pinched my nose and looked around. Empty soda cans of pop covered the floor. Open on the passenger seat was a map, with a big red circle drawn around the lake. Behind the seat were fishing rods and nets. But there was no sign of the shell.

Something grunted outside the van. I froze. Mom had said all the bison were back in the pen. Could she have been wrong? Had one escaped?

"Sam?" I whispered. "Was that you?"

Sam didn't answer. And then I spotted something pink and shimmery hanging from the mirror. *Aha!* The missing shell piece! I grabbed it and slid it into my pocket.

"Macy," a man's voice said. "Is that you?"

I turned around and found myself face-to-face with another park ranger. It was Mom's deputy, Mark.

"Get down here right now," he said. "I'm calling your mother."

Chapter Eight

Back at the lookout, Mom waited in front of the Jeep. Her hands were on her hips, and she was frowning. But with each step I took, I felt the piece of shell rubbing against my leg. This had been all worth it.

"Get in the Jeep," Mom said. She talked to Mark for a few minutes.

I slipped into the back seat. Sam was already in the middle, and Bug was on his other side.

"What happened?" Bug asked. "Mom is really mad at you."

"I found the missing piece," I said, pulling it from my pocket and handing it over to Bug.

"You went treasure hunting?" he stammered. "Without me?"

"You wanted to go birding," I said.

"But I thought I was part of your team," Bug said, his lips trembling.

"You are," I said, but Bug scowled and looked out his window.

Sighing, I put the shell back in my pocket. Mom's door opened, and I braced myself for her questions.

"Macy," she said as she climbed in. "What were you thinking?"

"We found the hole in the fence," I said. "I just wanted to see it."

"But I told you to stay away from there," she said. "And why were you in that van? Don't you know that's trespassing?"

"What do you mean?" I argued. "That van must belong to the vandals. You should be happy. I figured out who wrecked the fence."

Mom shook her head and turned to face me. "No, Macy, I am not happy. We don't know that the van and the vandalism are connected. But climbing into the van was very reckless of you. Not only did you put yourself in danger, but Sam too. What if the owner of that van had been in it? What if he'd gotten mad—or worse? You really gave me quite a fright."

I looked away. I wished I could tell Mom about MerKay, the Beast and the shell, but I had sworn on my handbook that I would not. Even if I hadn't, Mom would never believe me now.

Mom continued. "I don't know what to do with you except ground you."

"What?" I cried. "For how long?"

"One week. I want you to remember that when I tell you not to do something, I mean it."

"A week?" I said. "That's not fair! Summer is almost over."

"Well, maybe next time you will listen to me." Mom turned away and started the Jeep.

On the drive home I considered sneaking out that night after everyone had fallen asleep and letting Joy and MerKay know I had the missing piece. But if Mom caught me, what other awful punishment would she give me? Clean the public toilets? Shovel bison poop? Ground me for the rest of summer?

A darker thought occurred to me too. What if I *kept* the shell? Then would *I* be in control of MerKay? I shook my head. I'd sworn on my book to protect her. A deal was a deal. MerKay needed the shell.

Bug was still mad at me, but I needed his help.

"Bug," I whispered, "take this." I pulled the shell from my pocket and poked it into his side.

"What do you want?" Bug asked, swatting my hand away.

"You need to get this to Joy," I whispered.

Bug shook his head. "You do it. You like doing stuff by yourself."

"Bug," I hissed. "You know this is important."

He snatched the shell from my hand and hid it in his pocket. Then he ignored me for the rest of the way home. When we pulled into our driveway, I elbowed Bug in the ribs.

"Oh, uh, Mom," Bug said. "Can Macy take me to the beach? I think I left my bird book there."

Mom turned in her seat and looked from Bug to me. "No, Ben. I'm sorry. Macy is grounded."

"But I *need* it," Bug said. "I need to check on that bird I saw at the flats."

Mom sighed. Then she got an idea. "Sam, would you mind taking Ben? I can even pay you to watch him for an hour."

"*What?*" I said. "You never pay me to watch Bug."

Mom narrowed her eyes at me, and I quickly looked away.

"You don't need to pay me, Mrs. K.," Sam said. "I'll take good care of him, I promise."

As I watched Sam and Bug take off, a pang of jealousy stabbed me in the gut. I should have been the one taking the shell to MerKay. I'd taken all the risks. I had found the treasure. How many treasure hunters were prevented from enjoying their treasure because their moms had grounded them?

Waiting for Bug to get back was agonizing. I wanted to know everything that had happened and what MerKay and Joy were planning. But instead here I was, locked up like a common criminal.

I was lying on my bed, reading, when I heard him return. He stomped down the hall. He looked at me and then deliberately turned away. He slammed his bedroom door.

Clearly he was still mad. But I needed to know what had happened. I took a deep breath. I knocked softly on his door before pushing it open. Bug was on his bed, studying his bird book. He didn't look up.

He kept his eyes on the book, pretending I wasn't there.

"Listen, Bug," I said, sitting on the edge of his bed. "I'm really sorry I left you out of the plan. But I'm paying for it now. You know that Mom grounded me for a week, right?"

Bug put down his book. "A whole week is torture."

I nodded. For once we could agree on something. "And you would have been grounded too." That probably wasn't true, but I had to win him over. "So it's a good thing I didn't take you, right?"

Bug bit his bottom lip, then shrugged. "I guess so. But you shouldn't keep secrets, Macy. We're a team."

"You're right. And I'm very sorry. I won't do it again." I gave him a little side hug. "Will you tell me what happened, Bug? Was MerKay happy to get the shell piece back?"

"We didn't see MerKay," Bug said. "But we gave it to Joy and told her everything. She said to tell you to hold tight. She would think up a plan."

Hold tight? What did that mean?

I tossed and turned all night. I hated not knowing what was going on. In the morning I was really tired. And it turned out Mom had taken the day off work. *Great.* She said she wanted to get the house in order since we would be leaving soon. So first I washed the walls. Then she had me scrub the floors. Being grounded really sucked.

When it was lunchtime, Mom asked me to sit with her at the kitchen table.

"Macy," Mom said, "thanks for helping me this morning. I really appreciate it. And I know things haven't been easy. You always watch Ben when I'm at work, and I want to say thank you for that too."

I shrugged. "It's okay. He's not so bad. Most of the time."

"That's nice to hear," she said. "When we move to the city, things will be different. There are after-school programs that Ben can attend. You won't have to be on duty so much."

"But I don't *want* to move to the city," I said. "If I keep watching Bug for free, can we stay?"

"Macy," Mom said, "we've talked about this. You know this move isn't just about money. It's a great opportunity. For all of us. It might take some time, but I'm sure you'll come to love it."

"I won't love it," I said. "The city is like the deepest part of the lake. There are all kinds of things you can't see swimming around. In the city everything's new. I don't know any of the streets and I don't know any of the people. It's all just—too different!"

"I understand why you're nervous," Mom said. "But new places have new treasures. And I don't know anyone who likes to hunt for treasure as much as you do."

I crossed my arms, ready to argue some more, but there was a knock at the door. Mom got up from the table. I heard Joy's voice. I'd almost forgotten what she'd said about a plan.

"Hello, Macy," Joy said, coming into the kitchen. "I heard you got into some trouble last night."

"And now she's paying the price," Mom said. "No treasure is worth putting yourself and others in danger."

"I'm stuck here, grounded," I said.

"Well, you're in luck," Mom said. "I was just telling Joy how hard you've worked this morning. She needs help to fix a broken railing at her boathouse."

I looked away. My face was warm. If Mom only knew the truth.

"I could really use an extra set of hands," Joy said. "What do you think?"

I looked from Joy to Mom. "So am I still grounded?" I asked.

"Why don't you help Joy out this afternoon," Mom said. "And then we'll talk."

"Deal!" I said, racing to grab my shoes at the front door. "Let's get to work!"

Chapter Nine

MerKay was waiting for us in the boathouse. "Thank you so much for finding this piece," she said, holding the pink shell to her chest. "When we get the rest of it back, I can return home."

"Okay, kids," Joy said, turning to us. "Everyone has a job to do. Sam and Ben, I want you two to take a look at that book on the history of the Buffalo Pound area." She pointed to the bookshelf. "Macy might be onto something. Maybe there's a reason the Beast is here. See if you can find any clues."

She turned to me. "Macy, I do want your help fixing the rail. It's not safe. But there's a bigger reason. I find that keeping my hands busy helps my brain solve puzzles. And this is a big puzzle."

"And I am going to keep looking the best way I know how," MerKay said, handing the shell back to Joy. "Please keep this safe for me," she added and slid back into the water.

While Sam and Bug stayed in the boathouse to do research, Joy and I unloaded wood from her truck. Then she opened her shed, which I had never been in before. Like most sheds, it was filled with hammers, saws and other tools. But there was also a shelf against the far wall filled with the coolest stuff. A stack of maps, a compass and a book called *Archaeology Adventures*.

"Archaeology is kind of like treasure hunting," Joy said when she saw me looking at the book. She crossed her arms and leaned against the door.

"You were a treasure hunter?" I asked.

"Still am," she said. "Once a treasure hunter—"

"—always a treasure hunter," I finished. "Why didn't you say so sooner?"

"Back in my day, not many girls were treasure hunters," she said. "But I've been watching you, and I've noticed you turn in a lot of lost treasures at the Trove."

"Thanks," I said. My face was getting warm again. "I saw your pictures in the boathouse. Did you find treasure all over the world?"

Joy nodded. "Yes, I did. But some of my favorites were found here in Canada. You never know what you can find right in your own backyard."

We both looked at the boathouse and laughed. A mermaid had to be the greatest find of all time.

"Now let me teach you some carpentry," Joy said. "It's a skill every good treasure hunter should have."

We set up a sawhorse on the deck and got to work. Joy showed me how to measure and mark for my cut and even let me use her saw. While we cut a new length of railing and posts, we talked about the Beast and where it could be hiding. We had just started the repair when Sam and Bug appeared.

"No luck," Sam said. He slumped down at the open end of the dock. He kicked off his sandals and stuck his feet in the water.

"I guess we're not that good of treasure hunters," said Bug sadly.

"Nonsense," said Joy. "You kids just need a break." She looked at me. "Macy, we need one last thing to finish the railing." She put down the hammer. "I want you to go back to the Trove. Tell the Captain we need eight six-inch bolts to secure these posts." She stopped and winked at me. "That way, no one will accidentally break the railing again."

"But what if my mom—" I started.

"It's rail-building business," Joy said. "She'll understand. But you must go straight to the store and back. No side treasure-hunting jobs. Deal?"

"Deal," I said, joining Bug and Sam.

"Good," she said. "I think I'll go up and make myself a cup of tea. Oh, wait a second." She popped into the boathouse. "Take this with you." Joy tossed the shell at me. "You never know when you'll find the other half."

On the way to store, Bug and Sam told me what they'd learned from the book. Nothing that seemed like a clue to the Beast though.

"There must be some place we haven't thought of," I said.

When we got to the store, it was locked again. That seemed even weirder this time. It was the middle of the day!

"Come on," I said. "Let's go around back."

A pail of rocks propped open the screen door to

the Captain's quarters. I knocked on the door, but no one answered.

"He's probably way back in that storage room again," Bug said.

We walked inside and headed toward the storage room, calling out for the Captain. We opened the door. The room was dark and lined with way more boxes than before. But there was no sign of the Captain, so we walked to the end of the room and through the door that opened into the store.

The store was empty. "Captain?" I called out. "Anyone here?"

"What should we do?" asked Sam.

"I guess it would be okay if we found the bolts and left a note and some money," I said, moving toward the counter. I was thinking that if Mom saw the great job I'd done on the railing, she'd "unground" me. Then I spotted something shocking.

"You guys," I whispered. "Look!"

Sitting on the shelf, right next to the Captain's ship in a bottle, was the missing shell. I ran over for a closer look. The Captain had found the shell!

As I reached for it, I bumped the ship in a bottle off its stand. The bottle rolled toward the edge of the counter. Just before it rolled off and crashed to the floor, Bug grabbed it.

"Good job, Bug!" I said.

"I owed you one after smashing the shell bottle," he said, carefully putting the Captain's boat in a bottle back on its stand. I watched him turn the bottle and then lean in closer.

"Whoa, Macy. Take a look at this!"

Bug pointed to the bow of the tiny ship. I read the tiny painted letters of the ship's name.

The Beast!

Chapter Ten

"We need to get out of here," I said, slipping the shell into my backpack.

"Not so fast." The voice came from behind us. It was the Captain. "What are you kids doing in here?" He did not sound friendly at all

"You left the back door open," I said. My mind raced. How was the Captain connected to the Beast? Had he been hiding MerKay's shell from us all along?

"And we were—we were looking for you," Sam said quickly.

"Well, here I am," the Captain said, holding his arms out at his sides.

"We need some bolts," I stammered. "Six-inch ones. Eight of them."

"They're for a railing," Sam added. "At Old Lady Wilson's place."

The Captain frowned, looking past me to the ship in a bottle. "What are you doing over there?"

"Just checking out your ship," I said, blocking his view so he wouldn't see that the shell was missing. "I've never seen it up close. What happened to it again?"

The Captain's face darkened. "You mean I've never told you kids about how I lost my ship one dark night? A bad storm came out of nowhere, and it sank," he said. He seemed agitated and clearly wanted us out of there. "Now what was it you said you needed? Bolts? I've got some over here."

He moved to the front section of the store and starting putting bolts in a bag.

"I noticed your boat is called *The Beast*," I said.

"The Beast?" Sam said, eyes wide.

"It was a crabbing boat," the Captain said. "And a tough one. The storm that night was just too rough—almost supernatural..." The Captain's voice trailed off as he stopped filling the bag.

"Where is it now?" I asked.

The Captain shook his head and turned back to us. "Somewhere deep in the Pacific, off the coast of Vancouver Island. It never had a chance against those monstrous...waves."

I glanced at Sam and Bug, but they looked too scared to move.

"Thanks for these," I said, grabbing the bag of bolts the Captain held out. "Can you put it on Mrs. Wilson's tab? We better get going. She's waiting for us."

We headed for the door, but the Captain stepped in front of us before we could escape. "Hold on a minute.

I need to talk to you kids about that shell you found," he said.

My heartbeat went into overdrive. I held my breath. *Think, Macy, think.*

"I got hold of Drake," the Captain said. "The shell wasn't stolen. Someone claimed it the same day you brought it in."

He was lying! Thankfully, the air that escaped my lungs sounded like a sigh.

"And I'm sorry," the Captain added. "But they didn't leave any reward money."

"That...sucks," I said.

The Captain nodded, then opened the door for us. "You better get going. You don't want to make Old Lady Wilson even more grouchy." He winked.

The three of us ran through the open door to freedom.

Chapter Eleven

It didn't take us long to bike back to Joy's cabin. I couldn't wait to tell her we'd found the other part of the shell! And see what she thought about the newest clue Bug had discovered. But as we got closer to her cabin, I spotted Mom's patrol car. We slowed to a stop and looked at one another. I hoped I wasn't in bigger trouble for leaving Mrs. Wilson's property.

We ditched our bikes near the patrol car and walked slowly toward the cabin. Mom's voice drifted from Joy's porch.

"So it's not your fish?" Mom asked.

"No," Joy said. "I rescued it."

"And the person you *rescued* it from took it back?" Mom asked. "This all sounds, pardon the expression, a bit fishy."

"Well, really, they *stole* it back," Joy said. "It wasn't theirs to begin with."

Mom sighed, a sound I was getting all too familiar with. "Joy, I don't understand. Why didn't you call me the moment you found out someone had brought a fish from out of province without a license? It's my job to handle these things."

"I hadn't gotten around to it yet," Joy said. "I was planning to inform you this week. But then I realized that the fish was missing. There's evidence of a struggle."

"Okay," Mom said. "Let's take a look."

What was going on? Had someone taken MerKay? We had just been with the Captain. So if he wasn't the Beast, who—or what—could it be?

"Hi!" I squeaked out as I rounded the cabin. I held up the bag of bolts. "We're back with the supplies."

"Hi, kids," Joy said. Her forehead was scrunched with worry. "Thank you for getting those. But we have a problem. My *fish* is missing."

Mom turned around. A frown lined her face. "Have you kids seen this fish?"

I slowly nodded. "Yes, we have."

"We were helping Mrs. Wilson protect it," said Sam.

Mom shook her head. "I can't believe you kept this from me. It's against the law. Even if you thought you were rescuing it."

"Sorry, Mom," I said. "We thought we were helping."

Mom closed her eyes and took a deep breath. Then she turned back to Joy. "Show me the boathouse."

The padlock was on the floor. The door was wide open, and the place was a mess. I felt sick. What had happened?

"You kids stay outside," Mom said.

Mom and Joy went inside while Bug, Sam and I stood in the doorway. Joy's desk had been knocked over. Her books were all over the floor, and so were the scales that had been on the desk. Mom leaned over and picked one up. It was as large as a clamshell and fit in her palm.

Gradually the scale changed from a shimmery blue-green to the color of her hand. Mom stared in disbelief. "Exactly what kind of fish was this?" she asked.

"Uh…well, I'm not exactly sure," Joy said. "I was always better with the names of artifacts than of marine life."

Mom raised an eyebrow, then turned to us. "Describe the fish for me."

"It was large," I stammered.

"Yeah, and it had a long tail," Bug continued.

"And really spiky fins," Sam added.

Mom's eyes narrowed. "A large fish with a long tail and spiky fins." She turned to Joy. "What is really going on here, Joy?"

I stepped forward as Joy's head dropped. "It's not her fault, Mom. Sam and I snuck in here yesterday."

"I lost my soccer ball," Sam added. "We were just trying to find it."

"You broke into Joy's boathouse?" Mom asked, looking from Sam to me to Bug. "And you dragged your little brother into this?"

Bug shook his head. "I was looking for birds."

Mom threw in her hands in the air. "Macy, what does any of this have to do with the missing fish?"

"It wasn't Joy's fault we found the fish," I said. "That's all."

"We will talk about this later," Mom said. "Now go home and wait for me. Right now I need to take Joy to my office for a statement. There are laws at this lake to not only protect the people, but also the wildlife."

I turned around and walked past Sam and Bug. Man, Mom was pretty upset with me. I wondered how long I would be grounded for now.

When I stepped off the dock, I realized I was still holding the bag of bolts. And I hadn't told Joy the most important thing! "Joy," I said, turning back, "here are the bolts for the railing. Sorry it took us so long. The Captain was telling us about his old ship, *The Beast*. Did you know he used to catch crab in the Pacific Ocean?"

Joy took the bag from me and raised an eyebrow. "How interesting. Thanks, Macy." Then she leaned in and whispered, "We'll talk soon."

We watched Mom drive away with Joy in her patrol car. I would eventually have to face Mom. But right now MerKay needed us. With Mom busy with Joy, it was the perfect time to try to find MerKay and the Beast ourselves.

Chapter Twelve

"I can't believe MerKay is missing," I said. "What do you think happened?"

"I don't know," Sam said. "But the boathouse looked like a gruesome crime scene!"

"We'll never find her now," Bug said.

"Never say never, Bug," I said. "What do we know so far?"

"I thought the Captain was acting pretty weird at the store," said Sam. "And when Bug saw that the boat was called *The Beast*, it occurred to me that maybe the *Captain* is the Beast. But how could he possibly have gotten from the boathouse to the store before us?"

"Yeah, I thought that too at first," I said. "But even if he got here super fast, where would he have put MerKay?"

"What about that big tank he had?" Bug asked. "I didn't see it in the store today."

"That's right!" I said. "Bug, you're brilliant! I bet he put the tank back in that old truck at the bison pen. We need to find it again."

The ground vibrated, and all three of us moved to the side of the road as a large cube van sped past. The driver looked *very* familiar.

"Did you see what I saw?" I asked Sam.

"Yes! That driver looked a lot like Drake McDaniel!"

"And that van is big enough to hold a tank!" I added.

We sped after the van as fast as we could. We saw it go down a dirt path just before the turnoff for the store. It stopped behind a row of trees where the road turned into a path. I knew that path—it ran downhill to the beach. The driver slid out of the front seat, tossing a soda can onto the ground. I stopped dead in my tracks, making Sam and Bug brake abruptly behind me. It was Drake. What was he up to?

Dropping my bike at the side of the road, I scurried behind a tree. Drake continued down the path toward the lake. This was our chance to see what was in the van!

I ran up to the back of it and pulled on the door handle. It was stuck. Bug and Sam grabbed on too, and we finally got it open. Inside was the Captain's large fish tank. But it was empty.

"No," I said, stepping back from the van. "That doesn't make any sense. Where's MerKay?"

"Look!" Bug said, pointing down to the beach.

Drake was kneeling at the end of the boat dock. It looked like he was checking a rope tied around the post. Then he leaned down and looked into the water. After a few minutes he stood and walked back toward the van.

"Hide!" I said. I ducked behind the trees. Bug and Sam followed. The three of us squeezed together.

As Drake approached the van, he slowed down. *Oh no!* I'd left the back door open. He checked inside, then looked over his shoulder. I held my breath. If Drake found us, what would we do?

Drake shrugged. He slammed the door shut, then climbed back inside and drove away.

"That was too close," Sam said.

"Let's see what he's hiding in the water," I said, running down the path.

At the end of the dock, Sam and I pulled on the rope while Bug leaned down to look. "It's MerKay!" Bug cried. "She's trapped in a net."

"We'll save you," I called to MerKay. Even with her being underwater, I could see that her eyes were big and wide. She looked terrified.

Sam and I tried to untie the knots, but they were too tight. I stood up, looking for something that could help us cut the net. There was nothing.

"Hold on, MerKay," I said. "We're going to help you." Treasure-hunting rule number five: Never leave a teammate behind. Running back to my bike, I yelled to the others, "You guys stay with MerKay, and I'll go get Mom. She'll know what to do."

Chapter Thirteen

I had never ridden so fast in my life. I wished I had a phone! But Mom had said no way, not until I could pay for it myself. As I came closer to the Trove, I had a crazy idea. I didn't want to go anywhere near the place again, but it *did* have a phone. Help would come that much faster if I could call my mom. I checked. The old pickup wasn't there, and I didn't see the cube van either. Maybe this would work.

I would just have to take a chance.

I reached the door and carefully swung it open so it wouldn't squeak. No one was inside. *Whew!*

But then the Captain popped up from behind the counter. I nearly jumped out of my skin. "Well, hello there, Macy. What can I do for you? More treasures to show me?"

Think fast, Macy. Think! "Uh, I need to call my mom," I said. "It's...it's a lake emergency."

"Of course. Let me get the phone." The Captain turned and rummaged the back counter. He turned back with a cordless receiver in his hand.

"You know, I noticed something missing from my shelf." He passed the phone to me.

"Oh yeah?" I said. I wasn't really listening. Obviously he wasn't suspicious, or he wouldn't have given me the phone. I quickly punched in Mom's cell number.

"Yes." The Captain's voice got quiet. "And I think you know where it is."

Oh no. I raised the phone to my ear. There was no tone. *Oh no.*

"Um...er..." I tried to say something, but the Captain was coming out from behind the counter. "I can explain..."

"There is no need. I suspect you and your friends found something much more valuable than a shell, didn't you?"

I quickly punched in the number again and put the phone to my ear. Nothing. I lowered the phone and looked at the counter. The phone base was unplugged.

And the Captain now stood between me and the door.

"I'd like that shell back, please," the Captain said menacingly.

I threw the phone at him and ran toward the storage room.

"It's no use, Macy. You can't run from me," the Captain called.

Inside the storage room, I hid behind a tall wall of stacked boxes and tried to move slowly toward the door to the Captain's bedroom.

"I'll tell you what, Macy," the Captain said. "I'm feeling generous. You want money. I need that mermaid. How much money do you want for the shell? That way no one gets hurt. Well, no one human, that is."

"I know you're the Beast!" I cried. "And I will never betray MerKay!" The door to his quarters was so close. I needed to make a run for it.

"Oh, there you are!" he said, popping into view. "Give it up, Macy. I've got you now."

I pushed a tall stack of boxes at the Captain. They toppled over, hitting another stack. And then another. Soon dozens of boxes were crashing down on him.

This was my chance! I raced for the door and ran through the Captain's quarters. The pail of rocks was still holding the outside door open. *Freedom!*

"Not so fast!" Drake said, blocking the way to my bike. The pickup truck was parked behind him. "I told you nosy kids that I'm a master hunter." He slapped a coil of rope against his palm. "Now it's time to shut you up for good."

I grabbed the pail of rocks and chucked it at Drake. Then I ran toward the lake and the private dock. The gangplank was my only hope. I climbed the ladder as fast as I could. I had almost reached the top when Drake grabbed hold of my sandal.

"I've got you now!" he cried.

I kicked him. Hard. He slipped and fell down the ladder. I climbed out onto the gangplank. I carefully walked to the end. I looked down at the dark water and shuddered. I looked back behind me. Drake was halfway back up the ladder again. And now the Captain was there too.

I was trapped!

Chapter Fourteen

"Macy," the Captain said. "It's time to give up. We've got you cornered."

"That's right," Drake said, crawling onto the gangplank behind me. "You'll never jump. We know you're afraid of the water."

"I'm not afraid of the water," I said, turning back to the lake. "I just don't like not knowing what's in it." Way down the beach I could see two small figures on a dock, waving their arms. Sam and Bug! Could they see me?

Something shimmered just below the surface. It was MerKay! I glanced over my shoulder one last time. Drake was coming toward me fast. I took a huge breath and jumped.

The cold lake water surrounded me, but this time I didn't panic. I calmly swam back up to the surface. MerKay was right beside me.

"The mermaid, Captain!" Drake cried out overhead. "She's escaped again!"

MerKay took my hand, and we swam away faster than I'd ever swum before. The power of her tail and fins pushed us through the water like a speedboat. We were on our way to the dock she had been tied to. Sam and Bug jumped up and down as we approached. MerKay helped me out of the water and then turned to leave.

"MerKay, thank you so much for saving me back there," I said.

"No, thank you. If you hadn't been so brave in the first place, I would never have gotten free."

"I have something for you," I said. I took off my very soggy backpack and handed over MerKay's two shell pieces. She squealed with joy as she put them together. With a shimmer, the shell welded itself together.

"Now I can go home!" MerKay said. "We should let Joy know what's happened. Why don't I take you all to her cabin?" I was thrilled at the idea of another high-speed ride.

Just then the Captain came racing down the beach toward us. He was holding a big net. Drake was right behind him.

"Run!" I yelled to Bug and Sam. I made it off the dock and started down the beach. Sam caught up to me. But where was Bug? I looked back and realized the Captain was right behind him. Sam and I both ran back, just as the Captain tossed his giant net into the air. It landed on top of all three of us, catching us like fish.

"Get over here and help," the Captain called out to Drake. "This is all your fault."

Drake came into view. "*My* fault?" he hissed. "If it weren't for me, this entire plan would have fallen apart. I'm the one who thought of the fish tank for the mermaid. I'm the one who found a replacement van when the police took our old seafood van. *I* should be the *Captain*."

"Well, you're not," the Captain said. "You don't even have a ship!"

"You don't either," Drake said. "And you don't have the guts to get revenge on those mermaids. We never should have left the West Coast."

"What did MerKay ever do to you?" I asked through the net. I could see that MerKay was still nearby—her head popped up every so often. I was stalling as best I could while trying to think up a plan to get us out of this mess. "We need to keep him talking," I whispered to Sam.

"What did she do?" the Captain said. "I'll tell you what she did. She wrecked my life. Took away my livelihood."

"She's not strong enough to take down a ship," I said. "What really happened?"

"You want the truth?" the Captain asked. "One night when Drake and I pulled in our crab traps, we caught a mermaid. Imagine that! A real mermaid! What would you have done?"

"I would have helped her," Sam said. "Not kidnap her!"

"Well, I didn't have a choice," the Captain said. "That night the other mermaids attacked our ship. We woke up to find it sinking in the Pacific."

"So we fled to the mainland in a lifeboat," Drake said.

"Why did you take MerKay with you?" I asked.

"We had to," Drake said. "She was the only way we knew we'd get to land safely. Otherwise those monsters might have attacked us again."

"They attacked you because you had one of them!" said Sam.

"And then you didn't even let her go," I added.

"Once we got to land, I realized we couldn't," the Captain said. "We needed her to help us find the others. So we brought her as far inland as we dared to go and planned our revenge."

"We need to get out of here, *Captain*," Drake said.

The Captain glanced one more time in my direction. I scowled back. These two were nothing more than dirty kidnappers. And now they were adding kidnapping three kids to their rap sheet.

"When my mom catches you, you're going to be sorry," I said.

"Yeah," said Bug. "You don't want to mess with her."

"No one is getting hurt," the Captain said, holding up a hand. "I swear. Before we disappear, I'll take you back to the store and leave you inside. Just tell me where the shells are."

"We don't have them," I said. "She does."

Right on cue, MerKay rose from the water. She held her shell to her lips, and a low humming filled the air. I motioned for Bug and Sam to cover their ears. I just knew it wasn't a sound we should hear. As the humming got louder, the Captain and Drake slowly turned and started moving toward the lake. They continued walking, right into the water, until it was up to their waists. What was MerKay going to do? Drown them?

"Stop!" I called to her. "You don't want to do this. You're not a monster. Let them go!"

MerKay took the shell away from her lips and disappeared under the water.

"Hurry up," I said to Bug and Sam. "We need to get out of here before it's too late."

MerKay's spell didn't last long. Drake started shaking his head, then pulled at the Captain's arm. "Wake up!" he said. "Those kids tricked us." He turned toward us and yelled, "You little brats are going to be sorry!"

Then I heard Mom's voice coming from the trees. "Stop right there."

The Captain froze, but Drake ran out of the lake and down the beach, headed toward the store.

"Get him!" Mom said. Two other rangers chased down Drake while Mark grabbed the Captain.

Mom raced to the bottom of the hill. "Are you all okay?" she asked, pulling the net off us.

"We are now," I said.

"You kids could have been seriously hurt," Mom said, taking the three of us into her arms. "Or worse."

"We had to save the mer—the fish," Bug said.

"Joy kept trying to tell me this story about a how the fish was kidnapped by a beast," Mom said. "It made no sense. But when she mentioned you had told her a Beast was at the Trove, I got a terrible feeling that you kids hadn't gone straight home like I'd asked."

"I'm sorry," I said. "It's all my fault. But like Bug said, we had to try to save the fish."

"Where is it now?" Mom asked.

I looked out into the lake. "It's finally free."

Chapter Fifteen

The inside of Joy's cabin was just as interesting as the boathouse. She had pictures and artifacts from all over the world. It was amazing!

"One day you could visit these places too," Joy said. She pointed to a world map hanging on her living-room wall. Pins marked all the places she'd traveled to.

"Especially now that you're ungrounded," Mom added.

Even though I had helped catch the Captain and Drake, I had still broken the rules. I'd been grounded for two weeks. But it hadn't been all bad. Sam had stopped by to play soccer most days. Bug had kept me updated about birds and bugs he'd spotted at the lake. I'd even done some treasure hunting in our yard. The lake was ten thousand years old. There were a lot of treasures buried around here!

"It's too bad we're moving next week," I said. "We won't see you again."

Joy laughed. "Don't be silly. I go into the city all the time. I'll come visit once I'm back from my trip. Now, stop worrying about things you can't control. Race down to the boathouse. I've got a surprise for you. I'll meet you there."

The three of us ran across the lawn to the boathouse and swung open the door. Inside, MerKay waited next to an old canoe.

"Joy wants you three to explore the lake while she's away," MerKay said, holding out her arms.

"Cool!" Sam said, stepping into the canoe.

"We could row all the way to the flats in this," Bug said.

"It's a great way for you to get out on the lake," MerKay said to me. "The lake is no different than the land. It's filled with lots of treasures."

"I don't know," I said. "The canoe looks pretty tippy to me."

MerKay shook her head. "Macy, you only have one week left at the lake. Do not miss this opportunity to explore."

I sighed. MerKay was right. It was time I got used to the unknown. We were moving to the city soon. The practice would do me good.

"Do you really have to leave?" Sam asked. "Can't you give us a tour of the lake first?"

MerKay sighed. "I wish I could. I have enjoyed getting to know you all. But I miss my family more than anything. It's time for me to return to the ocean."

MerKay said goodbye to Sam and Bug, then turned to me. "Macy," she said, "you're braver than you realize. Look at everything you've done since we met. You found my shell. You stopped the Captain and Drake. And you made the big leap off the gangplank, even though you were really scared. Trust yourself. I am sure you will come to love the water as much as I do."

I nodded. "I'll try. I promise."

We heard Joy's and Mom's voices getting close to the boathouse.

"That's my signal to leave," MerKay said.

"Wait," Bug said. "We need to know one thing. How did you get the shell into the bottle?"

"Magic," MerKay said. Then she winked and disappeared into the water, leaving behind a tiny ripple that surrounded the canoe.

"What's going on in here?" Mom asked from the doorway of the boathouse. Joy stood next to her.

"Nothing," I said. "Why do you ask?"

"I thought you were getting a surprise," Mom said.

As Sam and Bug showed Mom the canoe, Joy pulled me aside. "Before I forget," she said, reaching for a rolled-up piece of leather on her desk, "these are for you. These last few weeks with you kids have made me realize that you're never too old for an adventure."

I unrolled the fabric, revealing a set of archaeology tools. "Why don't you see what you can dig up in the city," Joy said. "I think you'll be pleasantly surprised."

"Thank you!" I said, giving her a hug.

The four of us stood in Joy's driveway and waved as she drove away.

"That woman sure has led an interesting life," said Mom.

Sam, Bug and I looked at each other and smiled. Mom had no idea how interesting.

Chapter Sixteen

My hands pushed off the ledge in the deep end of the city's outdoor pool. I put on my snorkel and dove with the rest of my scuba-diving class.

MerKay had taught me not to be afraid. A true treasure hunter is an explorer at heart. I live in the city now. Once I started checking out the different streets, stores and parks, I realized that the city wasn't scary at all. Plus, I was finding tons of cool treasures all over this place. City people were always losing their things!

At the end of the class, I quickly packed up my diving gear and headed home. On my way I walked past my new favorite store, The Early Bird. It had treasures from all over the prairies. And Bug loved its wildlife photos. The only thing it was missing was ice cream. But I didn't have time to stop today. Joy was back from her trip. And she was bringing Sam with her to the city for a visit!

"How was the west coast?" Mom asked Joy.

"Wonderful!" Joy said. "I did some sightseeing. I saw the ocean. I even saw an entire school of—a pod of killer whales. A once-in-a-lifetime event." She turned from Mom and winked at me.

"They never found that strange fish," Mom said. "And the weird thing is, I couldn't find anything in the database that matches those scales. Can you kids describe it for me again?"

"Big," I said.

"Yeah." Bug nodded. "With a long tail."

"And spiky fins," Sam finished.

Mom sighed. "Well, they've got people watching the lake now. The poor thing won't likely survive for long out of its natural habitat."

"How's your new job going?" Joy asked, changing the subject. "Any word on Drake and the Captain?"

"I imagine they'll be behind bars for a long time," Mom said, standing up. "It's one thing to transport a fish without a license. But to try to kidnap three kids? They must have been involved with a smuggling operation. Why else would they take a risk like that?" Mom slipped into the kitchen. "Anyway, it's all behind us now. Does anyone want more iced tea?"

"Yes, please, Mrs. K.," Sam said.

Joy leaned over and whispered loud enough for the three of us to hear. "MerKay is very grateful. She sent these as a thank you." Joy passed each of us a glass bottle with a different sea souvenir inside. Mine had a sand dollar.

"What's that?" Mom asked, returning with the iced tea. She picked up my bottle and tipped it upside down. The sand dollar clinked. "How did they get this inside the bottle?"

"Magic," said Bug, Sam and I, all at the same time.

Acknowledgments

Thanks to my children, who are always on the lookout for stories about girls on adventures; my husband, for taking our girls on adventures so I could have my writing time; my mother, who continues to support my writing in every way possible by reading every draft I toss her way; old friends Jennifer Bardsley, Jamie Kramer and Arthur Slade, who gave early feedback on this story; and new friends like Paul Coccia, who convinced me that getting a book deal in Canada was possible and helped me polish my pitch.

I'm especially grateful to my editor, Tanya Trafford, who not only saw potential in my story but also strengthened my manuscript extensively. Thank you too to all the staff at Orca for making this dream come true.

DEAD MEN TELL NO TALES

DEATH BY AIRSHIP

Orca currents

Arthur Slade

Swashbuckling
pirates rule the skies!

"FILLED TO THE BRIM WITH HUMOROUS
DIALOGUE AND VIVID ACTION SEQUENCES."
—CM: Canadian Review of Materials

Melanie McFarlane is the author of several otherworldly adventure novels for kids and teens. When not writing, she's on the lookout for mermaids and other fantastical creatures while prepping for the zombie apocalypse. She lives in Moose Jaw, Saskatchewan, with her family.

For more information on all the books

in the Orca Currents line, please visit

orcabook.com.